Ladybird  Readers

Let's Make Dumplings

Series Editor: Sorrel Pitts
Text adapted by Hazel Geatches
Activities written by Kamini Khanduri

LADYBIRD BOOKS

UK | USA | Canada | Ireland | Australia
India | New Zealand | South Africa

Ladybird Books is part of the Penguin Random House group of companies
whose addresses can be found at global.penguinrandomhouse.com.
www.penguin.co.uk   www.puffin.co.uk   www.ladybird.co.uk

Penguin
Random House
UK

First published 2020
001

Printed in China

A CIP catalogue record for this book is available from the British Library

ISBN: 978-0-241-40185-9

All correspondence to:
Ladybird Books
Penguin Random House Children's
80 Strand, London WC2R 0RL

MIX
Paper from
responsible sources
FSC® C018179

Ladybird Readers

Let's Make Dumplings

Based on the
Masha and the Bear TV series

Picture words

Masha

Bear

Panda

dumplings

dough

roll (verb)

cut (verb)

butterflies

caterpillar

jar

pot

Bear and Panda were hungry. Panda wanted to make dumplings.

First, they got some dough.

Panda rolled the dough.

Bear cut the dough and
made balls with it.

Then, Panda rolled the balls.
Bear got the meat.
It was fun!

Masha was outside. She wanted to catch butterflies.

Then, she saw a caterpillar.
"Hello, little caterpillar!
You can be my friend!"
she said.

She could not catch the
caterpillar. It was too quick.

The caterpillar ran to Bear's house. Masha ran to Bear's house, too.

The caterpillar jumped into Bear's kitchen.

Masha jumped into Bear's kitchen, too.

Then, the caterpillar ran on the table.

Masha ran on the table, too. Panda was not happy.

Masha caught the caterpillar, and she put it in a jar.

"You can stay here," she said.

Then, Masha saw the dough. "Oh!" she said. "I want to play with it!"

Panda was not happy.

Masha played
with the dough.
She made a bird.

Then, she
made some
sausages.

Then, she
made a face!

"This is fun!"
said Masha.

Panda and Bear were angry. They wanted to make dumplings.

"I want to make dumplings, too!" said Masha.

Panda made small and beautiful dumplings.

Masha made big and ugly dumplings!

Panda cooked the dumplings.

Then, Masha remembered
her caterpillar. "Oh no,
where is it?" she thought.

Masha and Bear looked in
lots of pots, but they could
not find the caterpillar.

Then, Bear looked in the
blue pot. What did he find?

Bear found lots of butterflies!
"Oh, butterflies!" said Masha.
She was very happy.

Then, Bear and Panda could eat their dumplings. They were very happy, too!

Activities

The key below describes the skills practiced in each activity.

Spelling and writing

Reading

Speaking

Critical thinking

Preparation for the Cambridge Young Learners exams

1 **Match the words to the pictures.**

1 Masha

2 caterpillar

3 Bear

4 butterflies

5 Panda

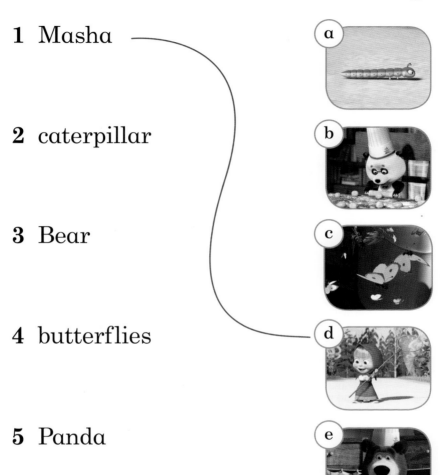

2 **Circle the correct words.**

Bear and Panda were hungry. Panda wanted to make dumplings.

1 Bear and Panda were in the

   a kitchen.   **b** garden.

2 There was a book on the

   a window.   **b** table.

3 Panda was

   a angry.   **b** hungry.

4 He wanted to make

   a dumplings.   **b** cakes.

3 Ask and answer the questions with a friend. 💬

First, they got some dough.

Panda rolled the dough.

Bear cut the dough and made balls with it.

1

> *What did they do first?*

> *First, they got some dough.*

2 What did Panda do?

> *He . . .*

3 What did Bear do?

> *He cut . . .*

4 **Circle the correct words.**

Then, Panda rolled the balls.
Bear got the meat.
It was fun!

1 Panda rolled the **(balls.)** / **meat.**

2 **Bear** / **Panda** was on a chair.

3 Bear got the **chair.** / **meat.**

4 They **wore** / **made** hats.

5 It **were** / **was** fun!

5 Circle the correct answers.

1 Where was Masha?

  a She was inside.

  b She was outside.

2 What did Masha want to catch?

  a Butterflies and then a caterpillar.

  b Caterpillars and then a butterfly.

3 Could Masha catch the caterpillar?

  a No, it was too quick.

  b Yes, it was slow.

6 Complete the sentences. Write a—d.

1 Masha wanted   d

2 Then, she saw   ....

3 She could not   ....

4 It was   ....

a too quick.

b catch the caterpillar.

c a caterpillar.

d to catch butterflies.

7 **Look and read. Write *yes* or *no*.**

The caterpillar ran to Bear's house. Masha ran to Bear's house, too.

14

The caterpillar jumped into Bear's kitchen.

Masha jumped into Bear's kitchen, too.

15

1 The caterpillar ran to Bear's house. ....yes........

2 Masha ran to Panda's house. ....

3 The caterpillar jumped into Bear's bedroom. ....

4 Masha jumped into Bear's kitchen. ....

8 **Write the correct verbs.**

Then, the caterpillar ran on the table.

Masha ran on the table, too. Panda was not happy.

16

Masha caught the caterpillar, and she put it in a jar.

"You can stay here," she said.

1 The caterpillar **(run)** .... ran .... on the table.

2 Panda **(be)** .... not happy.

3 Masha **(catch)** .... the caterpillar.

4 She **(put)** .... it in a jar.

5 "You can stay here," she **(say)**

....

9 **Read the text. Choose the correct words and write them next to 1—4.**

1 run	running	ran
2 to	too	two
3 catches	catch	caught
4 can	can't	could

The caterpillar [1] ....ran........

on the table. Masha ran on the table,

[2] .... Panda was not

happy. Masha [3] .... the

caterpillar, and she put it in a jar.

"You [4] .... stay here,"

she said.

10 **Look at the picture and read the questions. Write the answers.**

Then, Masha saw the dough. "Oh!" she said. "I want to play with it!"

Panda was not happy.

18

19

1 What did Masha see?

She saw the .... dough ....

2 What did Masha want to do?

She wanted to ....

3 Who was not happy?

....

40

11 Look and read. Put a ✓ or a ✗ in the boxes. 📖 ✿

1  This is dough. ✓

2  This is a bird. ☐

3  These are dumplings. ☐

4  This is a face. ☐

5  These are sausages. ☐

12 **Read the text. Choose the correct words and write them next to 1—5.**

> played   were   made   make   is

Masha [1] ..... played ..... with the dough. She made a bird. Then, she [2] .... some sausages. Then, she made a face. "This [3] .... fun!" said Masha. Panda and Bear [4] .... angry. They wanted to [5] .... dumplings.

13 Talk about the two pictures with a friend. How are they different? Use the words in the box. 💬

> Masha big beautiful making
>
> dumplings ugly small Panda

> *Panda is making dumplings in picture a. Masha is making dumplings in picture b.*

14 **Circle the correct pictures.**

1 You can eat these.

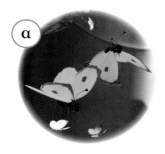

2 This is small and green.

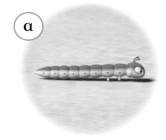

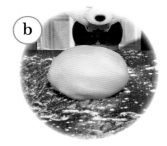

3 You can cook things in this.

15 **Read the text and choose the correct words.**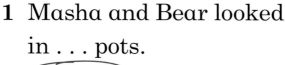

1 Masha and Bear looked in . . . pots.
   a lots of
   b a few

2 They . . . find the caterpillar.
   a could
   b could not

3 Then, Bear looked in the blue . . .
   a jar.
   b pot.

4 . . . did he find?
   a What
   b When

16 **Write the correct sentences.**

1 (lots) (found) (of) (butterflies) (Bear) (!)

Bear found lots of butterflies!

2 (happy) (Masha) (very) (was) (.)

....

3 (very) (too) (They) (happy,) (were) (!)

....

17 **Look at the letters. Write the words.** 📖 ✏️ ⭐

noufd

1 Bear _____found_____ lots of butterflies.

fertubeltis

2 "Oh, _____!" said Masha.

paphy

3 She was very _____.

olduc

4 Then, Bear and Panda _____ eat their dumplings.

rewe

5 They _____ very happy, too!

Ladybird Readers